Acting Edition

MW01615651

She Kills Monsters

by Qui Nguyen

ISBN 978-0-573-70564-9

www.concordtheatricals.com
www.concordtheatricals.co.uk

MUSIC AND THIRD-PARTY MATERIALS USE NOTE

IMPORTANT BILLING AND CREDIT REQUIREMENTS

SHE KILLS MONSTERS received its world premiere Off Off Broadway at The Flea Theater in New York City on November 4, 2011, under artistic director Jim Simpson, producing director Carol Ostrow, and managing director Beth Dembrow; with scenic and lighting design by Nick Francone, sound design by Shane Rettig, costume design by Jessica Pabst, puppet design by David Valentine, choreography by Emily Edwards, fight direction by Mike Chin, prop design by Kate Sinclair Foster, and stage management by Michelle Kelleher. The director was Robert Ross Parker. The cast was as follows:

AGNES	Satomi Blair
TILLY	Allison Buck
CHUCK	Jack Corcoran
MILES	Bruce A. Lemon
KALIOPE/KELLY	Megha Nabe
LILITH/LILLY	Margaret Odette
VERA, EVIL GABBI, THE BEHOLDER	Brett Ashley Robinson
NARRATOR, EVIL TINA, FARRAH THE FAERIE	Nicky Schmidlein
STEVE	Edgar Eguia
ORCUS/RONNIE	Raúl Sigmund Julia

CHARACTERS

(6F/4M)

AGNES

TILLY

CHUCK

MILES

KALIOPE/KELLY

LILITH/LILLY

VERA, EVIL GABBI, THE BEHOLDER

NARRATOR, EVIL TINA, FARRAH THE FAERIE

STEVE

ORCUS/RONNIE

*Note: All actors play monsters when needed.

SETTING

Athens, Ohio, and the imaginary land of New Landia.

TIME

1995.

NOTE ON STAGING

Because of the many short scenes, it is recommended that all scene transitions should be done "seamlessly" with small light adjustments instead of any full blackouts to help the play move along briskly.

Prologue

(Lights come up on a hooded female NARRATOR who speaks a lot like Cate Blanchett in the "Lord of the Rings" movies. Orchestrated music plays in the background as she weaves her tale.)

NARRATOR. In a time before Facebook, World of Warcraft, and Massive Multiplayer Online RPG's, there once existed simply a game. Forged by the hands of nerds, crafted in the minds of geeks, and so advanced in its advanciness it would take a whole second edition to contain all its mighty geekery.

And here in the land of Ohio during the year of 1995, one of the rarest types of geeks walked the earth.

A Dungeon Master without fear, prejudice, or a penis. This nerd was a girl-nerd, the most uncommon form of nerd in the world and her name was Tilly Evans.

(Lights come up on TILLY EVANS, a teenage girl decked out in full leathery D&D fantasy armor with a cool-ass sword in hand. She is surrounded by a horde of Kobalds [goblin-like creatures].)

(Suddenly they attack!)

(TILLY quickly slays each of the monsters with grace and efficiency.)

(She stands poised over their dead bodies as the NARRATOR continues...)

But this story isn't about her...
This story is about her sister...

(Spotlight on AGNES EVANS.)

(The following sequence is presented elegantly in either shadow-play or with shadow-puppetry.)

NARRATOR. Agnes Evans grew up average. She was of average height, average weight, and average build. She had average parents and grew up in the average town of Athens, Ohio with her little sister Tilly.

Tilly however was anything but average.

TILLY. What are you doing?

AGNES. Talking on the phone. What are you doing?

TILLY. Trying to re-animate a dead lizard with the power of electricity.

AGNES. Oh, okay... WHAT!?!

NARRATOR. Though they shared the same parentage, the two girls had very little in common. Agnes being of average disposition was into more typical things such as boys, music, and popular television programs while her sister Tilly became fascinated with the dark arts – magic, dragons, and the vanquishing of pure evil.

*(**AGNES** goes to put a CD into a stereo.)*

*("**ACE OF BASE**"* starts playing.)*

TILLY. EVIL!

*(**TILLY** smashes the stereo with her sword and runs away.)*

NARRATOR. As Agnes grew and grew, she became more and more engrossed with transcending her seemingly permanent state of averageness and made one grand wish on the night of her college graduation that she would forever regret.

---

*A license to produce *She Kills Monsters* does not include a performance license for Ace of Base. The publisher and author suggest that the licensee contact ASCAP or BMI to ascertain the rights holder to acquire permission for performance of any Ace of Base song. If permission is unattainable, the licensee should create an original composition in a similar style. For further information, please see music use note on page 3.

*(**AGNES** looks up to the Gods...)*

AGNES. I wish my life was less boring!

(Her wish echoes...)

NARRATOR. And so the Gods answered her wish by smiting down every single member of her family in a car crash.

(The shadow puppet of car crashing into a tree.)

(As it does, the tree transforms into a dragon and flies away with the broken vehicle.)

(Fade to black.)

But this isn't the story of those tragedies.

It is a story about how Agnes, the girl who never left home, finally found a way out...

(Projection: She Kills Monsters.)

Scene One

(Lights come up on **CHUCK**, *a nerdy teen dressed like a Grunge Rocker roadie. He's wearing large headphones, a flannel shirt tied around his waist, and jamming out to Beck's loser as he's working the counter of a "RPG gaming store.")*

CHUCK. *(Singing to himself.)*

SOY UN PERDEDOR

I'M A LOSER BABY, SO WHY DON'T YOU KILL ME?

*(***AGNES** *enters and pokes his shoulder which startles him!)*

WHOA, WHAT IN THE HADES!

AGNES. Sorry, I didn't mean to scare you –

CHUCK. I wasn't scared. I'm a black belt...in Jedi...jitsu –

AGNES. I'm looking for a Chuck Biggs?

CHUCK. You're looking at him! But my hommies just call me simply DM Biggs cause, you know, I'm "big" where it counts.

AGNES. Uh...

CHUCK. As in MY BRAIN!

AGNES. *(Relieved.)* Oh!!!

CHUCK. Not because I'm fat.

Seriously, it really has nothing to do with body mass index, I actually work out...or plan on working out –

AGNES. I get it.

CHUCK. So what can I do for you?

AGNES. Someone told me you might know a thing or two about Dungeons and Dragons.

CHUCK. Depends if we're talking first or second edition... PSYCHE! It doesn't matter which edition cause my D&D IQ is plus three hella high!

AGNES. You're very odd.

CHUCK. "Odd" as in hot, right?

AGNES. No.

CHUCK. So what do you want to know about the D and the D?

AGNES. Well, I have this thing. I'm not quite sure what it is.

CHUCK. Well, lemme checkity check it out!

*(**AGNES** hands **CHUCK** the notebook.)*

AGNES. Be careful with it. It's not mine.

*(**CHUCK** takes it and carefully begins leafing through the pages.)*

You know, you're not exactly what I was expecting.

CHUCK. What? Were you expecting some nerd? 'Cause I'm no nerd.

I got a girlfriend.

From New York.

AGNES. How did *you* meet someone from New York?

CHUCK. *(Proudly.)* On a little thing I like to call… THE INTERNET! You've been on the Internet, right?

AGNES. We have it at work.

CHUCK. It's the bomb, right?

I got it hooked up at my house. Top of the line. I'm talking 56 kilobits per second! Blazing fast. If you ever want to come over and check it out…

AGNES. I'm good.

So about the notebook…

CHUCK. Well, it's clearly a homespun module.

AGNES. Clearly. What's that?

CHUCK. It's like a map for a D&D game. An adventure. And this one looks like it's written for one to two players at entry level skills and power designations with –

(Something stops him.)

Yo, hold up. Where'd you get this?

AGNES. It's my sister's.

CHUCK. Your sister is Tillius the Paladin?

AGNES. Who?

CHUCK. Tilly Evans.

AGNES. You knew her?

CHUCK. Of course I knew her. Every player here in Athens has been on a campaign with her. And she was your sister?

AGNES. IS my sister.

CHUCK. Oh man, I'm sorry – I didn't realize –

AGNES. So can you help me figure out what it all means?

CHUCK. Sure, but –

Look, I should tell you something up front now that I know who you are.

Nothing can happen between us, okay?

I know you were vibing me and all when we first met, but now that I know who you are, it would be disrespectful.

Plus you're like wicked old and that would be creepy.

AGNES. Okay.

CHUCK. So if you're cool that –

AGNES. I'm cool.

CHUCK. Then I can help you. So what do you want to do with this module exactly?

AGNES. Well, Chuck, it's a game, right?

I want to play it.

Scene Two

(Lights come up **MILES** *standing in* **TILLY**'s *bedroom.)*

MILES. So this is all that's left to pack?

AGNES. Yep.

MILES. It's a lot.

AGNES. Yep.

MILES. So is this exactly how –

AGNES. Yep.

Exactly the way she left it –

MILES. Your sister was a slob.

AGNES. She was sixteen.

MILES. She was a sixteen-year-old slob.

AGNES. Where do I even begin with all this?

*(***MILES*** picks up a He-Man action figure.)*

MILES. Man, your sister was really into some geeky shit.

AGNES. Yep.

MILES. You sure you don't want any help?

'Cause you know I'm strong, right?

Like bull.

AGNES. You're also clumsy.

Like ass.

MILES. I'm not clumsy.

AGNES. Should I remind you of my former coffee table?

MILES. It was faulty design.

AGNES. Thanks for the help, babe, but you should go. I should pack this myself. I'm her sister, it's part of the job.

MILES. You sure?

AGNES. Positive.

MILES. Alright then, I'll just go ahead start moving some of your boxes over to OUR new place.

AGNES. That sounds like a good plan...just don't drop anything.

MILES. I love you.

AGNES. I love you too.

> (**MILES** *give her a kiss.*)

AGNES. Now go.

> (**AGNES** *gives him a smile and rushes him out the door.*)
>
> (*She suddenly drops the "loving girlfriend" act.*)

Sorry about that. Are you still here? Chuck?

> (*Suddenly, with awesome lights, sound, and smoke effects, a hooded* **CHUCK** *rises from behind a kitchen table where he's been inexplicably hiding the whole time.*)
>
> (*As he talks, he drops his wannabe b-boy persona and begins speaking all "wizardly."*)

CHUCK. Greetings, Adventurer! I am Chuck Biggs also know as DM Biggs and I will be your Dungeon Master!

AGNES. You'll be my what?

CHUCK. SIT!

AGNES. Okay.

CHUCK. Before you is a game. A game like no other. One written to test your mind, your cunning, and your badassness.

There's also chips and soda for your snacking enjoyment. But lay off the Twizzlers, those are mine. Are. You. Ready?

AGNES. Um, I guess?

CHUCK. Then imagine if you will this setting.

> (*Suddenly, a spotlight falls on* **AGNES** *as everything goes dark around her.*)

You are standing on the sands of a mystical beachside. To one side of you is the endless ocean, on the other is an ominous dark forest.

And from the distance, a hooded stranger approaches.

(A spotlight falls on a **HOODED FIGURE.***)*

AGNES. Okay. Am I supposed to do something here? Like fight it?

CHUCK. Not yet.

AGNES. But you said a hooded stranger approaches. If a hooded stranger approached me in real life, I would mace him.

CHUCK. You don't have mace here.

AGNES. So what do I do?

CHUCK. Just chill.

I'm still giving you your given circumstances.

AGNES. Sorry.

CHUCK. So you're on a beachside with a dark forest to your right and the endless sea to your left...and then –

> *(The* **HOODED FIGURE** *turns to* **AGNES** *and walks towards her.)*
>
> *(***AGNES** *awkwardly raises her fists in a fighting position to ready herself.)*

TILLY. Welcome to New Landia, stranger. I am –

> *(The* **STRANGER** *pulls back her hood and reveals herself to be –.)*

AGNES. Tilly?

TILLY. Tillius actually. The Paladin.

AGNES. You're in this game?

TILLY. Of course I am. I made it up, didn't I?

> *(Overwhelmed by seeing her sister,* **AGNES** *immediately goes to hug her.)*

AGNES. Tilly –

> *(***TILLY** *stops her though.)*

TILLY. *(Coldly.)* This is a D&D adventure, not therapy.

> **(AGNES** *backs off.)*

AGNES. Sorry.

TILLY. So are you sure you want to do this?

AGNES. I do. But I don't know exactly what I'm doing –

TILLY. Of course you don't. You're a noob.

AGNES. But I do WANT to do this, Tilly. I know this all this meant a lot to you so I just want to –

> **(TILLY** *does not react to this at all.)*

Right. "This isn't therapy."

> **(TILLY** *looks* **AGNES** *up and down to see if she indeed is serious about playing D&D.)*

TILLY. Okay, big sis.

If you really want to play,

then let's play.

But first you're going to have to meet the rest of our party.

AGNES. What party?

TILLY. Every adventurer has a party. This one's ours. Cue the intro music. Go.

> *(Badass* Matrix-*y style music begins playing.*[*]*)*

> *(Suddenly, a leather-clad warrior* **LILITH** *appears in a spotlight. Think* Underworld's *Kate Beckinsale but with more skin showing. Besides being crazy hot, she sports red eyes, fangs, and wields a very large demonic-y battle axe.)*

First up is Lilith Morningstar.

Class: Demon Queen.

---

[*] A license to produce *She Kills Monsters* does not include a performance license for music from *The Matrix*. The publisher and author suggest that the licensee contact ASCAP or BMI to ascertain the rights holder to acquire permission for performance of any *Matrix* music. If permission is unattainable, the licensee should create an original composition in a similar style. For further information, please see music use note on page 3

AGNES. What in the hell is she wearing?

TILLY. She acts as our squad's muscle. Whenever you're surrounded by an armada of Ogres, she's the one you want holding the steel. She is a perfect combination of both beauty and brawn.

LILITH. Violence makes me hot.

> *(Another spotlight falls on a very pale-skinned and white-haired elf. She's tall, lean, and armed with an elaborately decorated wooden staff. She looks like a supermodel.)*

TILLY. Next up is Kaliope Darkwalker.
Class: Dark Elf.

AGNES. Seriously, does no one here like wearing all their clothes?

TILLY. Along with her natural Elvin agility, athleticism, and ass-kicking abilities, she's also a master tracker, lock-picker, and has more than a few magical surprises up her non-existent sleeves. No pointy-eared creature has ever rocked so much lady hotness.

KALIOPE. I'm in the mood for danger.

> *(**KALIOPE** joins **LILITH** and they begin posing all sexy.)*

TILLY. And then there's –

AGNES. Pause! CHUCK!

> *(Reality suddenly shifts back to the kitchen table.)*

CHUCK. Yeah, what's up?

> *(**AGNES** points to the girls who are all suddenly frozen like figurines.)*

AGNES. What is this?

CHUCK. This is your party.

AGNES. My party is a leather-clad dominatrix and an Elvin supermodel?

CHUCK. Dude, don't look at me. This is what your sister wrote.

AGNES. "Violence makes me hot."

CHUCK. Okay, so there's definitely a certain amount of improv involved, but I swear this is the gist of what Tilly created.

AGNES. This?

CHUCK. Yes. This.

AGNES. My sister wrote this?

CHUCK. Look, do you want to play the game or not?

AGNES. Sure, whatever.

(CHUCK *throws his hood back on.*)

CHUCK. And then –

TILLY. There's me. I'm the brains of this operation.
Name: Tilly Evans aka Tillius the Paladin, healer of the wounded and the protector of lights.
Class: Awesome.

(TILLY *steps up beside* KALIOPE, *and* LILITH. *They fall into a movie poster-esque pose together.*)

(CHUCK*'s Dungeon Master voice booms over them from the heavens.*)

CHUCK. Welcome to the Quest for the Lost Soul of Athens. Your mission is find and free the Lost Soul before it is devoured by the dark forces of darkness forever.

(*All the girls high-five each other.*)

AGNES. Seriously, you guys are supposed to be a team of badasses?

(*Suddenly, three monsters rush in growling and snarling.*)

(*In a fast and impressive series of moves,* TILLY, KALIOPE, *and* LILITH *slay them.*)

Okay, nevermind.

KALIOPE. Curious. What form of creature is this?

LILITH. Can I eat it?

TILLY. Lilith, you said you were quitting.

LILITH. I said I'd cut down. I've only had two this week.

AGNES. Cut down doing what?

KALIOPE. Eating the flesh of bad guys.

AGNES. Ew.

KALIOPE. Why are you dressed so strangely?

AGNES. I'm dressed strangely? You do know you look like a Thundercat, right?

TILLY. Elf!

KALIOPE. Yes, Noble Paladin Tillius –

TILLY. Any word on Orcus's location?

AGNES. What's an Orcus?

LILITH. Is this your special skill? Asking questions? Yes, that will come in handy.

AGNES. What's your special skill? Being a –

TILLY. Guys, stop it.

Orcus is a demon overlord of the underworld. If there's a lost soul, he'll either have it or at least know where it is. Kaliope is our tracker. If he's near, she'll know his location.

> (**KALIOPE** *pulls out a map and places it on the ground for all to see.*)

> (*They all crouch down to look at it.*)

KALIOPE. The entrance to the cave of Orcus is at the next bend. But unfortunately neither Lilith nor I can accompany you for no magical creatures are allowed into his lair unless they risk being entrapped there forever.

> (**AGNES** *is examining* **LILITH**'s *costume.*)

AGNES. Seriously, there has to be more to this outfit, right?

LILITH. You look like you would be delicious with a side of baby.

> (**LILITH** *snarls at* **AGNES** *which prompts her to run to* **TILLY**.)

AGNES. Okay! So we're going into a cave, let's go!

TILLY. Actually, Agnes, before we can go any further. We're going to have to equip you and build you a character. You can't just walk around looking like that.

AGNES. I'm not wearing what she's wearing.

TILLY. You're going to at least need a shield.

AGNES. A shield I can do.

TILLY. So what will be your alignment?

AGNES. My what?

LILITH. Are you good, lawful, chaotic, unlawful, evil?

AGNES. I'm a Democrat.

KALIOPE. And what will be your weapon?

AGNES. I guess a sword. A regular sword. Like yours.

TILLY. This is no regular sword.

KALIOPE. You have to earn a weapon like the one Tillius wields.

LILITH. The Eastern Blade of the Dreamwalker.

KALIOPE. Forged from the fiery nightmares of Gods.

LILITH. Blessed by the demons of Bricken.

KALIOPE. And bestowed upon the one who once banished the Tiamat from New Landia.

AGNES. So I can't have a sword like that one?

TILLY, LILITH, KALIOPE. NO!

AGNES. Fine, I'll just take a regular sword.

TILLY. And what will be your name?

AGNES. Agnes.

TILLY. No, what will be your character name?

AGNES. Agnes.

TILLY. Stop being an ass-hat, Agnes.

AGNES. No, I want to just use my name. Agnes.

LILITH. Fine, then it is decided, you are Agnes the Ass-hatted.

AGNES. That's not what I said.

KALIOPE. Agnes the Ass-hatted, welcome to our party.

Scene Three

(Cut to...)

NARRATOR. *(Voiceover.)* And so it was that Agnes the Ass-hatted and Tillius the Paladin ventured forth into the dark dwellings of the truly evil and quite large in stature, ORCUS THE OVERLORD OF THE UNDERWORLD, in search for the lost soul of Athens. But what they found deep in that cave was not what they were prepared for in the least...

> *(Inside a dark cave lit with only torches,* **ORCUS**, *an oversized red demon with large black devil horns sits reclined on a throne of skulls and bones. He is busy watching "Friends" on his demonic television set.)*

> *(***TILLY*** and* **AGNES** *quietly sneak in.)*

> *(***TILLY*** looks at* **AGNES** *and gives her a nod. The two girls jump out with weapons drawn.)*

TILLY. It is I, the great Paladin Tillius, healer of the wounded, defender of lights, and I have come here to –

> *(***ORCUS*** puts up a finger to shush her.)*

ORCUS. Shhhhhhh!

> *(***TILLY*** is confused.)*

AGNES. Um, we're here to fight you.

ORCUS. Yeah, that's not gonna happen.

TILLY. But we've come here to battle.

ORCUS. I know what you've come here to do and I'm telling you it's not gonna happen. I'm busy.

AGNES. This is the Overlord of the Underworld?

ORCUS. FORMER Overlord of the Underworld! I quit.

TILLY. You quit? You can't quit.

ORCUS. Whatchoo talking about I can't quit. You know how annoying it is to always get attacked by so-called adventurers all the damn time?

(An ADVENTURER named STEVE barges in.)

STEVE. Orcus! It is I, the great Mage Steve and I've come here to do battle!

ORCUS. See what I'm saying?

ADVENTURER. I've come to claim the Staff of Suh in the name of –

> *(ORCUS reaches over and grabs said Staff and tosses it over to STEVE.)*

ORCUS. Here ya go, little man. It's all yours.

ADVENTURER. Really, that's all I had to do? AWESOME!

> *(STEVE exits.)*

ORCUS. So what would you like? Treasure? Jewels? Some cheez-whiz? It's wicked good.

TILLY. I wish to free a soul.

ORCUS. Sure. Which one?

> *(TILLY bravely steps up to ORCUS.)*

TILLY. Mine.

AGNES. What?

TILLY. You heard me, Orcus. I want my soul back.

ORCUS. Coolio. And which soul would that –

> *(ORCUS takes a good look at TILLY.)*

Oh. Crap. This is a bit awkward.

AGNES. Wait, you're the lost soul of Athens?

TILLY. Orcus, can I have it back or not?

ORCUS. You're Tillius the Paladin, correct?

TILLY. Correct.

ORCUS. Yeah, this is a bit embarrassing but I sorta lost your lost soul.

TILLY. What do you mean you lost my lost soul?

ORCUS. Yeah, I mean I sorta traded it in for this badass TV/VCR combo from the, um, Tiamat.

TILLY. What?

ORCUS. Yeah, she was really into it and my old TV completely conked out in the middle of a Twin Peaks Marathon...

TILLY. So you just gave my soul to Tiamat?

ORCUS. TRADED your soul to Tiamat.

TILLY. For nothing?

ORCUS. Not for nothing. Have you ever seen Twin Peaks?

TILLY. Oh God.

AGNES. This isn't good, is it?

TILLY. No, not good at all.

ORCUS. Are you sure you don't want some Cheese-Whiz instead?

(Both girls glare at him.)

No? My bad.

Scene Four

(Cut to…)

*(**VERA** in her office. She's talking to a student.)*

VERA. Do you want an STD? No, you don't. At worst, that shit will kill you. In the least, it will get your shit itchy. And nobody likes a girl with an itchy hoo-hah. Now get out of here and keep your pants on! Stupid ass teenagers!

*(**AGNES** walks in and crashes in her chair.)*

Well, you look like shit.

AGNES. Thanks.

VERA. Crazy night with Miles?

AGNES. Crazy night. Not with Miles.

VERA. Well, do tell. Who's the new mystery man?

AGNES. It's not what you think. I was with a high school kid.

VERA. Say what?

AGNES. We were up all night… Role-playing.

VERA. Agnes, you know I'm all for experimentation and extracurricular activities, but maybe you should stick to guys your same age –

AGNES. JESUS, Vera, we were playing Dungeons and Dragons.

VERA. Dungeons and Dragons!?!

You know what? I think it was less weird when I thought you were playing Mrs. Robinson.

AGNES. You're like the worst high school guidance councilor ever.

VERA. No, I'm not.

(A student enters.)

STEVE. Hello, Miss Martin, I came by to ask you about –

VERA. Noooooooooooooo.

STEVE. Miss Martin?

VERA. Are you flunking out of a class?

STEVE. No.

VERA. Then you're fine. Come back later, I'm busy.

STEVE. Okay.

(The student exits.)

AGNES. I stand corrected, you should lead workshops on pedagogy.

VERA. And how does Miles feel about Dungeons and Dragons?

AGNES. You really don't like him, do you?

VERA. How long have you guys been together? Three years?

AGNES. Two…and, um, eighteen months.

VERA. See. And all he's done is asked you to move in with him? Please, son, keep your house, show me a ring!

AGNES. I'm not ready for that.

VERA. That's 'cause down deep you know that busted bustah is no good for you.

AGNES. Can we please change subjects?

VERA. So what's up with this game? Is this some sort of dorky quarter-life crisis?

AGNES. I know it's stupid, but… I'm just curious why Tilly liked it so much.

VERA. And?

AGNES. And I honestly don't see the appeal.

It's actually kinda mundane. All we've done so far is walk around and talk to things.

I thought there were supposed to be monsters in this game.

(Suddenly everything goes dark accompanied with a loud sound cue.)

Vera?

(VERA *is frozen. She doesn't respond.)*

Vera!

(Suddenly three giant insectoid-like bear creatures [Bugbears] enter the space.)

Oh crap…

Scene Five

(The monsters rush at **AGNES**. *She dodges out of the way as* **VERA** *disappears.)*

*(***CHUCK*** moseys into the space.)*

*(***AGNES*** runs up to him.)*

AGNES. What the hell's happening?

CHUCK. Three Bugbears are after you.

AGNES. Three what?

CHUCK. Three Bugbears.

AGNES. What the heck is a Bugbear?

CHUCK. What do you do?

AGNES. What do I do? I don't even know what a Bugbear is? Are they bugs? Are they bears?

*(***CHUCK*** sits back at his gaming table and rolls the dice.)*

CHUCK. You examine the Bugbears. They are neither bugs nor bears.

*(***TILLY*** enters.)*

TILLY. So this game is mundane, huh? All we do is talk and walk? You want more action?

AGNES. I didn't know things were suddenly going to jump out at us.

CHUCK. The first Bugbear strikes.

(It hits **AGNES***!)*

AGNES. OW! Wait, don't I get a turn?

TILLY. You wasted your turn examining the Bugbears.

CHUCK. Which they appreciate. Bugbears aren't used to getting such attention. The second Bugbear strikes.

AGNES. Don't roll that dice.

(A Bugbear strikes **AGNES** *in the face again hard.)*

OW!

CHUCK. You've been damaged.

AGNES. Really? I couldn't tell.

CHUCK. What do you do?

AGNES. I fight back!

TILLY. My character does the same.

> (**TILLY** *steps forward and impales her sword into one of the Bugbear easily killing it.*)

CHUCK. CRITICAL ROLL! Tillius slays one Bugbear.

> (**AGNES** *turns to one of the bugbears and raises her weapon.*)

You however swing –

> (**AGNES** *takes a swipe with her sword. The Bugbear dodges and smacks her in the face again.*)

AGNES. OW!!!

CHUCK. – and miss.

AGNES. What? Look at those things? How do I miss that?

CHUCK. The Bugbear strikes again.

AGNES. No, no, wait!

CHUCK. They miss.

AGNES. Okay, let me think.

CHUCK. You take a turn to think.

AGNES. No, I don't –

CHUCK. The other Bugbear strikes.

AGNES. Come on!

> (**AGNES** *tries to avoid the attack the best she can, but gets impaled by the Bugbear's weapon.*)

CHUCK. Huge damage! Agnes is down.

TILLY. Your character is dying, Agnes. What do you want to do?

AGNES. What can I do?

TILLY. Start playing this game correctly.

AGNES. What? How?

TILLY. Stop acting like a sarcastic ogre all the damn time and I'll help you. Can you do that?

AGNES. ...

TILLY. Agnes?

AGNES. Yes. Yes, I can do that.

TILLY. You promise?

AGNES. Yes, I promise.

> *(**AGNES** collapses to the ground.)*
>
> *(**TILLY** closes her eyes and hovers her hands over **AGNES**.)*

AGNES. What are you doing?

TILLY. Just shut up.

> *(Lights and sound indicate something awesome is happening.)*

CHUCK. Tillius uses a revive spell to restore all of Agnes's hit-points. You get back on your feet.

TILLY. We stand side-by-side and raise our weapons.

CHUCK. And this is what happens next –

> *(Hard-hitting music begins playing. An elaborate and badass fight ensues as the two girls work together to defeat their adversaries. **AGNES** fights impressively.)*

CHUCK. You've defeated the Bugbears! Agnes levels up! Gains plus one in being less of a dumbass!

AGNES. Wait, is that really a stat?

TILLY. Yep, totally is. You're less dumb! Yay! Now where's the rest of our team?

> *(Demonic **LILITH** and the **ELVEN KALIOPE** approach, forcing a reluctant **ORCUS** the Demon to walk with them.)*

LILITH. You're not serious, love. We're not actually going to bring Orcus along, correct?

KALIOPE. I must agree with Lilith, getting the worst demon in all the underworld to tote along with us does seem less than wise.

(ORCUS *raises his hand.*)

ORCUS. I totally agree. I am bad news. Look at me. I'm red. I got horns. I'm totes evil.

TILLY. No, you're coming with us.

ORCUS. Man, you're gonna make me miss "Quantum Leap."

TILLY. That's inconsequential.

ORCUS. Inconsequential? Have you seen Quantum Leap? The dude time travels...through time...by leaping INTO different bodies. Different BODIES, yo! And putting things right that once went wrong, and hoping each time that his next leap will be the leap home.

AGNES. That actually does sound interesting.

TILLY. You lost my soul, Orcus, so now you're going to have to help me get it back.

KALIOPE. He knows where your soul is?

TILLY. He gave it to The Tiamat.

LILITH. What?

(AGNES *raises her hand.*)

AGNES. Question. What's The Tiamat?

(TILLY *signals* KALIOPE *to tell her.*)

TILLY. This is Tiamat.

(*Using magic [aka a video projection],* KALIOPE *shows* AGNES *the dragon of legend.*)

KALIOPE. She is a five-headed dragon that has laid waste to generations of adventurers and civilizations since the dawn. Each of her heads embodies the five different elemental powers of the chromatic dragons – earth, fire, water, wind, and lightning. Many adventures have fought her. All have died.
All, except for one...

(KALIOPE looks at TILLY.)

AGNES. You fought that?

TILLY. Yes.

AGNES. That's –

TILLY. Useless. I didn't pull off killing her. And now she's stolen my soul for revenge.

(LILITH storms over to ORCUS.)

LILITH. And you just gave it away!?! I should rip out your insides and dine on them right here and right now, you overgrown sad excuse for a demonic entity!

(ORCUS looks LILITH up and down.)

ORCUS. Whoa, wait just a minute. Don't I know you?

(This stops LILITH dead in her tracks.)

LILITH. Um…what? No, you must be mistaking me for someone else.

ORCUS. No, I know who you are. You and me, we hang in the same evil underworld. And I don't think your daddy's gonna be too happy you're making time with a Paladin and a human.

AGNES. Who's her dad?

KALIOPE. The devil.

AGNES. That explains a lot.

(LILITH's demeanor suddenly shifts from total badass to shrinking violet.)

LILITH. Look, please don't tell him, okay? He'll kill me!

AGNES. Wow, suddenly you don't seem so tough.

(LILITH backhands AGNES sending her flying across the stage.)

ORCUS. Don't worry. He doesn't have any love for me either. Your secret's safe with me.

TILLY. Orcus, tell us the location of The Tiamat! Now!

ORCUS. Fine.

Go go Orcus Map!

(A comically large map suddenly appears out of nowhere.)

Behold my comically large map of New Landia. This is the path you will have to take if you want to face The Tiamat. You must first travel down the River of Wetness to the Swamps of Mushy –

AGNES. The names of these locations are terrible.

TILLY. I was going to go back and give them better names later, but – you know – I sorta died before I could get to it.

AGNES. Sorry.

ORCUS. Then you will climb the Mountain of Steepness to the Castle of Evil to find The Tiamat.

AGNES. Seems simple enough.

ORCUS. But to be able to face The Tiamat, you will have to face and defeat all three of its guardians, the Big Bosses of New Landia.

AGNES. That's less simple.

ORCUS. And each one of them are totally badass so – most likely – one if not all of you will die before you get there. So, yeah, you gotta do that...

OR we can chill out in my cave and rock us some Thursday Night Must-See TV!

Who's feeling me?

No?

Really, none of you guys are into ER? That Clooney Cat is a cutie!

(Knowing how dangerous this quest will be, noble TILLY *takes in a deep breath and addresses her party.)*

TILLY. My friends, I cannot ask for you all to come with me. The journey before us is too perilous and the prize too personal for me to expect you to risk your lives. I'm just one warrior and you all have so much ahead of you. Please if you do not wish to continue, you have my blessing to stay right here and be safe.

(Without hesitation, LILITH *takes* TILLY*'s hand.)*

LILITH. Tillius, you know as always you have my blade.

*(*KALIOPE *follows.)*

KALIOPE. And my staff.

ORCUS. Seriously, I'm totally fine with just chillin' –

TILLY. You don't get a choice.

ORCUS. Man!

KALIOPE. What about you, Agnes the Ass-hatted? What say you?

*(*AGNES *looks around at this crazy-ass team and smiles.)*

AGNES. Of course I'm in.

*(*AGNES *joins the party.)*

LILITH. Good. Then let us kicketh some ass.

NARRATOR. *(Voiceover.)* And so our team of adventurers set forth into the wild, following the path Orcus traced out for them. It was indeed treacherous and they did indeed kicketh ass...

(Music like LL Cool J's "Mama Say Know You Out"* kicks in! A high-energy montage of badassery happens here where we see our party kick ass by killing a a crap-load of different monsters in an assortment of different ways from badass to comedic. It is a cavalcade of D&D beasties. They behead mind flayers, slice up liches, smash umber hulks, crush bullettes, basically kill anything that would excite any geek who's ever played a fantasy game. It is gloriously violent and funny.)

---

* A license to produce *She Kills Monsters* does not include a performance license for "Mama Say Know You Out." The publisher and author suggest that the licensee contact ASCAP or BMI to ascertain the rights holder to acquire permission for performance this song. If permission is unattainable, the licensee should create an original composition in a similar style. For further information, please see music use note on page 3

(It culminates with a badass slow motion walk [á la Reservoir Dogs] *as the team wipes off monster blood and guts from their outfits.)*

Scene Six

(Lights come up on a beautiful **FAERIE** [**FARRAH**]*,
dancing and singing in the woods [Maybe to a
song like TLC's Waterfalls*].)*

*(***ORCUS*** approaches.)*

ORCUS. Aw, look at the little forest Faerie! Hello, little
Faerie, how are you?

*(***ORCUS*** *goes to pet* **THE FAERIE,** *but she
immediately decks him in the mouth.)*

OW!

FARRAH. Look, you overgrown sack of stupid, just cause
I'm pretty doesn't mean I won't fuck you the fuck up!
Seriously, did you see a sign on the way in here that
said "Petting Zoo"

ORCUS. No!

FARRAH. Then please do not try to touch me!

*(***FARRAH*** *pushes him to the ground.)*

ORCUS. I don't think I like that Faerie.

FARRAH. Now get out of my magically enchanted forest
before I decide to go all Faerie berzerker all over your
ugly asses.

AGNES. Hey, I thought fairies were supposed to be nice.

FARRAH. Nice? Yo, do I sound Canadian to you? Ain't no
one here gonna be nice all the damn time. Faeries are
happy. HAP-PY. No one said nice. And I'm brimming
like mad with some magical happiness. And guess what
makes me happiest? Kicking the crap out of any lame-
ass adventurers who decide to trespass on my magically
enchanted forest!

**A license to produce *She Kills Monsters* does not include a performance
license for "Waterfalls". The publisher and author suggest that the
licensee contact ASCAP or BMI to ascertain the rights holder to acquire
permission for performance of this song. If permission is unattainable,
the licensee should create an original composition in a similar style. For
further information, please see music use note on page 3

AGNES. Look, maybe we should just take the long way around to the mountain?

> *(Hearing where they're going suddenly makes* **FARRAH THE FAERIE**'s *wings perk up.)*

FARRAH. Whoa! Hold up. You're going to the mountain? As in the Mountain of steepness?

AGNES. As a matter of fact, yes.

FARRAH. Yo, I didn't know all that. You shoulda said something.

AGNES. We should've?

FARRAH. Y'all must be brave, right?

LILITH. We are.

FARRAH. Courageous.

KALIOPE. That would be an apt description.

FARRAH. So you're going to –

KALIOPE. Fight Tiamat.

LILITH. Vanquish the Dragon.

TILLY. And save my soul.

FARRAH. Man, sorry, I didn't realize all that –

AGNES. So are we cool?

FARRAH. Yeah, if I'd known all that, I woulda just killed ya right away instead of wasting my breath talking to ya.

AGNES. Um, say what?

FARRAH. I'm one of the great guardians, dummies.

KALIOPE. But she is but wee.

FARRAH. Yeah, and me and my wee butt is gonna kill the crap out of you guys!

AGNES. Seriously, what could she possibly do?

> *(***ADVENTURER STEVE*** *enters.)*

STEVE. It is I, the great Mage Steve, and I've come to –

> *(The* **FAERIE** *graphically rips out his throat in one quick move. He dies.)*

ORCUS. Yo, to hell with that noise. That girl is straight up cray cray!

> *(**ORCUS** tries to leave, but **TILLY** grabs him by the horn to stop him.)*

FARRAH. You've reached the end of your adventure. Time to die, dummies!

> *(**TILLY** pulls out her weapons. Her team follows suit.)*

TILLY. *(With a smile.)* I'll be your Huckleberry.

> *(From the heavens, **CHUCK** announces the fight like a ring announcer.)*

CHUCK. *(Voiceover.)* BOSS FIGHT NUMBER ONE: FARRAH THE FAERIE VERSUS TEAM TILLIUS.

> *(The **FAERIE** charges at the team of adventurers.)*
>
> *(Though she is indeed small and cute, she's a total badass and begins beating the crap out of the majority of **TILLY**'s party.)*
>
> *(**ORCUS** tries to smash her with his club, but she dodges and kicks him in his demon-balls. He curls over.)*
>
> *(**LILITH** and **KALIOPE** swing at her with their weapons, but like an elusive bug she maneuvers past them using what looks like a **FAERIE**'s version of Capoeira. When they miss, she counter-strikes each attacker with a kick to the head.)*
>
> *(**TILLY** tries to leap on her back, but she gets smacked in the face by one of the **FAERIE**'s wings.)*
>
> *(**AGNES** charges at the **FAERIE**, but gets tossd over its shoulder Akido-style.)*
>
> *(The heroes are in trouble.)*

KALIOPE. Our skills are no match.

(**LILITH** *looks over to* **TILLY** *and grabs her by the shoulders.*)

LILITH. We need magic. Real magic.

(**TILLY** *nods.*)

AGNES. Wait. What magic?

(**TILLY** *begins summoning a magic spell.*)

TILLY. I call on… MAGIC MISSILE!

(**CHUCK** *enters the space and announces –.*)

CHUCK. TILLY CASTS… MAGIC MISSILE!!!

(**CHUCK** *acting as the missile's puppeteer, sends a large fire ball across the stage in slo-motion.*)

FARRAH. Oh shit.

(*When the missile hits* **FARRAH**, *she slow-mo falls off stage.*)

(*Suddenly back in real time, an explosion of bloody* **FAERIE** *parts exlode onto stage.*)

AGNES. Aw gross.

Scene Seven

(CHUCK is chilling in AGNES's house when MILES enters.)

MILES. Agnes! Check it out, guess who just got the new Smashing Pumpkins double disk –

CHUCK. Dude, nice! But I'm not gonna lie, I much prefer the consistency of "Siamese Dream" over the gaudiness of "Mellon Collie and the Infinite Sadness."

MILES. Who the hell are you?

CHUCK. Oh, sorry, I'm Chuck. I'm Agnes's DM and you are?

MILES. You're her what?

CHUCK. Oh right, I'm not supposed to talk about that. I'm her friend. Her secret friend.

MILES. You're my girlfriend's "secret friend"?

CHUCK. Yeah, and you are?

MILES. Her boyfriend.

CHUCK. Oh yeah? I didn't know she was dating anyone.

MILES. Hold up, she didn't tell you about me?

CHUCK. Well, that's probably my fault. I keep her pretty busy if you know what I mean.

MILES. Keep her busy doing what?

CHUCK. Fighting monsters, my man. Fighting. Monsters.

MILES. I don't even know what that means. But I do know it means I sorta really want to punch you right now.

CHUCK. Why?

MILES. 'Cause she's my girlfriend!

CHUCK. No, man! It ain't like that. We just role-play!

MILES. You what!?!

CHUCK. Look, I got no feelings for her, okay? This is just for fun. I'm just here to help her play out this fantasy. There's no long term commitments!

MILES. Alright, I'm gonna break you in half, you son of a –
        (MILES grabs CHUCK and tries to put him in a headlock. However CHUCK's actually too big and strong.)

*(**MILES** ends up looking pretty silly trying to wrestle down **CHUCK** to no avail.)*

*(**AGNES** comes out of the front door, holding a pair of black leather gloves.)*

AGNES. Hey Chuck, sorry I'm late, but check out what I found! I think they'll help me stay in character...
(The two guys immediately separate.)

MILES. Hey.

AGNES. Oh, hi.

MILES. Um... I think I should go.

AGNES. Why?

MILES. You're clearly busy.

AGNES. Oh God, you know about this now, don't you?

MILES. Yeah, I'd say so.

AGNES. You don't think I'm a dork now, do you?

MILES. No, that's not what I'm thinking.

CHUCK. Hey man, you can join us if you want.

MILES. Say what?

CHUCK. I mean if you're comfortable. You could watch us for a bit and once you get a hang of it, just jump right in. I'll be easy on ya.

AGNES. Yeah, Chuck can be pretty rough.

CHUCK. Please, call me Biggs. Cause I'm big. Where it counts. So do you wanna play?

MILES. I'm gonna have to...bye.
*(**MILES** exits.)*

AGNES. I'll call ya later?

MILES. Wow, that dude really hates D&D.
(Seeing the gloves.)

Oooh, nice gloves!
*(**AGNES** shrugs and puts on her gloves. As she does, she's instantly transported to the D&D world.)*

Scene Eight

(AGNES enters back into the D&D world.)

AGNES. Tilly! Tilly, where are you? Check it out, I got myself some cool…

> *(As she looks around, she catches TILLY and LILITH in what looks like some sort of scuffle. The two girls are pushing and grappling with each other. It looks pretty physical.)*
>
> *(Seeing this, AGNES pulls out her blade and starts approaching.)*
>
> *(But before she reaches them, LILITH grabs TILLY by the head and starts aggressively…making out with her.)*

AGNES. Whoa, what the hell???

TILLY. Oh, hey there, Agnes. Nice gloves.

AGNES. What were you two doing?

TILLY. I was, uh…kissing my girlfriend.

AGNES. Whoa! Wait just a minute! You two are a couple?

LILITH. Does this upset you, lunch meat?

AGNES. It upsets me that you don't know how to put on all your clothes.

LILITH. I'd advise not talking to me in such a tone.

AGNES. And I'd advise wearing a complete shirt next time you're MAKING OUT WITH MY SISTER!

Oh, wait just a minute, I get it. You two are dating because "Tillius" is a guy character.

TILLY. Tillius isn't a guy character.

AGNES. Tillius is a guy's name.

TILLY. No. Tillius is a D&D name. I'm female, she's female, and we're lovers.

AGNES. So your character's gay?

LILITH. As am I.

(KALIOPE and ORCUS enter.)

KALIOPE. Me too.

ORCUS. I'm down with OPP ...as in penis. Not the other P. Ew.

AGNES. Wait, the big slacker demon is gay?

KALIOPE. As is everyone in New Landia. Well, everyone except for you, Agnes the Ass-hatted.

AGNES. Why is that?

KALIOPE. Well, maybe it's because you haven't met the right girl yet.

AGNES. NO, that's not what I meant. I mean, why is everyone here gay?

KALIOPE. Because it was the will of the creator.

AGNES. The will of the creator?

TILLY. Does that bother you, Agnes?

AGNES. Tilly, why'd you make everyone gay?

TILLY. Um, I don't know. If I were to take an educated guess, I'd venture to guess that maybe the author of this world was into wearing tanktops and The Indigo Girls.

AGNES. No.

TILLY. Yes.

AGNES. Noooo.

TILLY. Yeeees.

AGNES. NO! Wait. I need a time-out.

> (**AGNES** *walks away from the group.* **TILLY** *follows. They are alone together.*)

TILLY. Wow, I never took you for a homophobe.

AGNES. I'm not a homophobe!

TILLY. That's not what it looks like to me.

AGNES. I watch "The Real World," I listen to Madonna, there's no way I'm anti-gay.

TILLY. Then what's with the denial?

AGNES. What's with not giving your girlfriend a full costume?

TILLY. She's a she-devil.

AGNES. She's dirty.

TILLY. I didn't think this would upset you like it does.

AGNES. I thought I knew you, Tilly. At least good enough to know whether you dug boys or girls at this point in your life.

TILLY. You were busy.

AGNES. Not too busy to know this! Tilly, this is bullshit.
     I'm your sister. I shouldn't have to learn about you through a role-playing game.

TILLY. At least you're getting to learn something about me.

AGNES. …

TILLY. We should get back on the road.
     Are you coming?

AGNES. Fine.

TILLY. Lilith! Kaliope! Orcus!
     Where are they?

AGNES. Oh, it looks like they're over there, taking a nap.

TILLY. Elves and demons don't sleep.

AGNES. They don't? So I guess them being unconscious would be a bad thing, right?

>   *(Explosive lights and sound as two cheerleaders fly onto stage in an impressive musical number.)*
>
>   *(They look like normal cheerleaders, except they have all black eyes, bat wings, and blood all over their mouths.)*

TILLY. Oh crap.

AGNES. What?

TILLY. Succubus!

AGNES. Suck you what?

TILLY. Succubus. Demon girls from the demon world who like to do demonic things like sucking.

AGNES. Are they a boss?

TILLY. No. They're just really mean.

AGNES. So do we fight them?

TILLY. No, we run. GO!!!

> *(They try to run away, but* **TILLY** *gets cornered.)*

EVIL GABBI. Not so fast there, nerd.

> *(***TILLY***, though still dressed like her badass self, starts shrinking into her average everyday geek-girl persona.)*

TILLY. Hey guys, what's up?

EVIL TINA. Were you just looking at me?

TILLY. No. Not specifically. I was just looking, you know, in your general direction and then you stepped into my line of…fleeing.

EVIL GABBI. I think she's lying.

EVIL TINA. I hate liars.

TILLY. I'm not lying!

AGNES. Hey, what do you two think you're doing?

> *(***AGNES*** *marches right up to the two bullies.* **EVIL TINA** *however grabs* **AGNES** *by the throat and just holds her there.)*

AGNES. Ah!

TILLY. Let her go!

EVIL GABBI. I think the reason why she was looking at you, Evil Tina, is because she has the hots for you.

TILLY. That's not true.

EVIL TINA. Are you saying I'm ugly?

TILLY. No.

EVIL TINA. Then do you think I'm pretty?

TILLY. Uh…

EVIL TINA. I don't understand "uh." I don't speak "uh."

> *(***EVIL TINA** *begins bearing down on* **AGNES**.)*

AGNES. Owwww!

EVIL TINA. I don't speak "ow" either.

TILLY. No, I do I do! I think you're very pretty, you're so pretty!

EVIL TINA. Of course you think I'm pretty...dyke!

> *(EVIL GABBI, pretending to be nice, approaches the very scared and intimidated TILLY.)*

EVIL GABBI. Sorry, Evil Tina is just really sensitive about her looks.

EVIL TINA. Shut up, Evil Gabbi!

EVIL GABBI. She doesn't mean to be mean to you. I like you. I do. Do you want to join our club?

TILLY. What club is that?

EVIL GABBI. The awesome Evil Club!

TILLY. Uh...

EVIL TINA. Again with the "uh's"!

AGNES. Owwww!

TILLY. Okay, I would love to join.

EVIL GABBI. Okay! Sit right here and don't turn around.

> *(EVIL TINA and EVIL GABBI start whispering and laughing with each other as TILLY sits staring in the opposite direction.)*

> *(As she stands there, TILLY no longer looks like an awesome D&D warrior. She now just looks like a normal geeky teen getting picked on.)*

> *(She tries to sneak a peek.)*

EVIL GABBI. I said not to turn around, bitch!

TILLY. I'm sorry, I'm sorry.

> *(EVIL TINA and EVIL GABBI come up with a plan. They turn and look at TILLY with an evil smile.)*

EVIL GABBI. Okay, all you have to do to get into the awesome evil club is to make out with me for one whole minute.

TILLY. What?

EVIL GABBI. What do you say?

TILLY. Uh –

> *(Hearing "uh," EVIL TINA bears down on AGNES again.)*

AGNES. OWWW!

TILLY. Okay.

EVIL GABBI. Yummy.

> (**EVIL GABBI** *leans in.*)

> (**TILLY** *closes her eyes and leans forward to kiss* **EVIL GABBI**.)

> (*Suddenly, out-of-nowhere,* **EVIL TINA** *kicks* **TILLY** *in the face.*)

EVIL TINA. I knew you were gay!

EVIL GABBI. Hahaha. Dyke, you're so in love with me!

EVIL TINA. Here, why don't you make-out with your sister?

> (**EVIL TINA** *throws* **AGNES** *on top of* **TILLY**.)

EVIL GABBI. Oh God, you two are so gross.

> (**AGNES** *and* **TILLY** *works her way back up to her feet.*)

AGNES. And you two going to die!

> (*Both the* **SUCCUBI** *smile and begin laughing. Their laughter consumes* **AGNES** *and* **TILLY** *who fall to the ground laughing as well. The laughing becomes more hysterical as both* **TILLY** *and* **AGNES** *fall to the ground from painfully laughing so hard.*)

> (*It all suddenly stops.*)

> (*The* **SUCCUBI** *walk around looking at their victims.*)

EVIL TINA. See you around. Lesbians.

> (*The* **SUCCUBI** *girls skip away, holding hands.*)

> (**AGNES** *gets up and walks over to* **TILLY**.)

AGNES. Are you okay?

TILLY. No.

> (**TILLY** *runs away.*)

Scene Nine

(VERA's office.)

AGNES. Hey, Vera, you're not going to believe –

(AGNES *is stopped when she sees* LILITH *from the game sitting at* VERA's *desk. Except this* LILITH *is in regular school clothes and glasses.*)

LILITH. Sorry, Miss Martin just stepped out.

(AGNES *looks around to make sure she's not in the D&D game.*)

AGNES. What are you doing here?

LILITH. What do you mean?

AGNES. What are you doing here?

LILITH. I work here.

AGNES. You're real?

LILITH. Huh?

(AGNES *realizes she must sound crazy.*)

AGNES. Sorry, that must sound crazy.

LILITH. No, not at all...
So how can I help you?

AGNES. You just sorta look like someone I sorta...don't know.

LILITH. Yeah, I caught that.

AGNES. So where's Miss Martin?

LILITH. She's...uh... I don't know. She never tells me anything. She just handed me a bunch of papers to sort so, thusly, I'm sorting.

AGNES. You're a student here?

LILITH. What gave it away?

AGNES. I teach English III.

LILITH. Yeah, I know who you are. A bunch of my friends have you. I got Ms. Gates though.

AGNES. Delaine? Yeah, she's great.

LILITH. If you don't mind the smell of patchouli all the time.

AGNES. Tell me about it, she can stink out a teacher's lounge faster than Coach Francone.

LILITH. So you're, um… Tilly's sister, huh?

AGNES. You knew her?

LILITH. Well, sure. I mean I was in her class. You and I actually met two years ago –

AGNES. Oh right, you all came out to their…well, you know. That was really sweet of you guys to do that.

LILITH. She was awesome, Miss Evans. The best.

AGNES. Thanks.

LILITH. I loved her.

AGNES. What?

LILITH. We all did.

AGNES. I didn't catch your name.

LILITH. I'm Lilly.

AGNES. Wait, your name's Lilly?

LILITH. Uh, yeah.

AGNES. As in Lilith?

LILITH. Actually it's short for Elizabeth –

AGNES. So this was real.

LILITH. What was real?

AGNES. You and Tilly…you two were real.

LILITH. I'm not following –

AGNES. You two dated!

LILITH. WHAT? No!

AGNES. No, you can tell me.

LILITH. Look, Miss Evans, I didn't date Tilly! I like boys. I swear.

AGNES. No, this explains so much. Of course, you were together.

LILITH. No, we weren't.

AGNES. You don't have to hide it!

LILITH. I'm not.

AGNES. TELL ME!

> *(VERA enters.)*

VERA. Hey! What's with all the excitement?

AGNES. This is Tilly's girlfriend!

LILITH. No, I'm not!

VERA. Lilly, take my keys and go grab me a coffee, okay? Thank you, ba-bye!

> *(LILITH runs offstage.)*

Agnes, what are you doing?

AGNES. She was Tilly's girlfriend.

VERA. Okay, one, I don't think so. Two, even if she was, having a teacher basically scream out "you're a lesbian" in the middle of my office isn't the best way to coax her out of the closet. And, three, are those my gloves?

AGNES. Look, she might be the only link I have left to –

VERA. I know, Agnes. But, look at me, that is a seventeen-year-old girl who's been dating a member of that Athens High football team for over a year. If she's in the closet, she's in there deep.

Scene Ten

(Lights come up on TILLY. AGNES *approaches.)*

AGNES. Hey.

TILLY. Hey.

AGNES. What happened back there with the evil Cheer-o-stititutes?

TILLY. What did it look like?

AGNES. Did that sorta stuff really happen? I mean in real life?

TILLY. I was a dorky fifteen-year-old closeted lesbian, what do you think?

AGNES. So how come you had to make a game to tell me all this?

TILLY. I didn't want to tell you all this if that's what you're wondering. This game was supposed to be private.

AGNES. ...

TILLY. ...

AGNES. I met Lilly, by the way. The real one.

TILLY. Oh yeah?

AGNES. Yeah.

She's straight, isn't she?

TILLY. I don't know.

AGNES. It must have been hard.

TILLY. I guess.

AGNES. Tilly, you can talk to me –

TILLY. *(Suddenly out of character.)* I'm not really her, you know?

(CHUCK enters.)

AGNES. What?

CHUCK. I'm not her.

AGNES. Chuck?

CHUCK. Look, I can only extrapolate so much, but this is feeling a bit blasphemous.

AGNES. I was talking to my sister, do you mind?

CHUCK. Agnes, I'm all for role-playing, but this is a bit deeper than I usually get.

AGNES. Play the role, Chuck.

CHUCK. But Agnes –

AGNES. PLAY IT!

CHUCK. Okay. Look, there's something in here that I think you should see –

AGNES. Do it in character.

CHUCK. Agnes –

AGNES. DO IT!

(**CHUCK** *takes a deep breath.*)

CHUCK & TILLY. Agnes…

Can you do me a favor?

AGNES. What?

TILLY. I wrote something for Lilly. In here. Can you give it to her?

(**CHUCK** *pulls an envelope out from inside the notebook and hands it to* **AGNES.**)

AGNES. What is this?

CHUCK & TILLY. It's for her.

Scene Eleven

(**MILES** *enters* **VERA**'s *office.*)

MILES. Hey, can I talk to you for a minute?

VERA. What are you doing here?

MILES. I need advice.

VERA. Are you looking to return to high school?

MILES. No.

VERA. Are your grades slipping?

MILES. No.

VERA. Then I have nothing to advise you on. I'm a high school guidance councilor, Miles, not your therapist.

MILES. You're my friend.

VERA. No, I'm your girlfriend's friend. You, I don't like so much.

(**STEVE**, *a student, enters timidly.*)

STEVE. Hi, Miss Martin. Is this a bad time?

MILES. YES.

VERA. No. Come on in, Stephen.

STEVE. Hi.

MILES. Hey.

VERA. So what can I do for you?

MILES. Agnes is cheating on me with a high school kid!

VERA. I was talking to Stephen.

Stephen, how can I help you?

STEVE. Well, I was thinking about dropping out of the marching band, but scared it might affect my college applications since it's really my only extracurricular activity.

MILES. Kid, that shit don't matter.

VERA. Miles!

MILES. But you know what does matter? Your girlfriend hooking-up with a high school student!

VERA. Miles, have some perspective here! Can you see how this might be an inappropriate conversation to be having in front of a student.

STEVE. I agree.

VERA. Shut up, Stephen.

STEVE. Alright.

MILES. So what do I do?

VERA. Break up with her.

MILES. Really?

VERA. Yes, really. Be honest with me, Miles, it took you three years to even ask her to move in with you, it's not like you're that committed to her in the first place.

MILES. That's not true.

VERA. Stephen, if you were dating Miss Evans for three years – THREE years – what do you think the next logical step would be?

STEVE. Miss Evans? Well, she is really pretty.

MILES. Yo, what is up with high school boys digging on my girlfriend?

STEVE. I don't dig. I just acknowledged.

VERA. What would you do, Stephen?

STEVE. I...uh... I guess I'd ask her to marry me?

VERA. See what I'm saying?

MILES. Who asked you?

STEVE. Miss Martin did.

MILES. Well, it doesn't matter either way, because she's cheating on me.

VERA. Miles, she's not cheating on you.

MILES. I met him. She admitted it. He's her "secret friend."

VERA. Yeah, I know.

MILES. You know?

VERA. He's her Dungeon Master.

MILES. He brings her into a dungeon?

VERA. Jesus Christ, Miles, NO! He's a D&D dork. He's the guy who rolls the dice and whatever.

STEVE. Actually, in a typical D20 scheme, the adventurer is actually the one who should be rolling the dice –

VERA. Shut up, Stephen.

MILES. She's playing D&D?

STEVE. Miss Evans plays D&D? Wow. Cool.

MILES. Don't you even think about it, kid.

STEVE. Um, so about my conundrum.

VERA. What conundrum?

STEVE. About the marching band.

VERA. Oh right. Yeah, that stuff doesn't really matter. Get back to class.

STEVE. Thank you?

MILES. You really suck at your job.

VERA. And you really suck at being a boyfriend.

STEVE. Well, I think you both suck.

(**STEVE** *exits.*)

MILES. So she's just playing D&D? That's it? Why?

VERA. Well, maybe you should ask her.

Scene Twelve

KALIOPE. What's wrong, Agnes the Ass-hatted? By the droop of your shoulders and your downward gaze, it would indicate you are troubled somehow.

AGNES. Wow. Observant.

KALIOPE. Was that sarcasm?

AGNES. No.

KALIOPE. My apologies, Agnes. We Elves may have heightened speed, agility, strength, and attractiveness –

AGNES. And you're also humble to boot.

KALIOPE. We're unfortunately lacking in "emotional awareness."

AGNES. So you're like a robot?

KALIOPE. No, we're Elves. We're above emotions. That's a human trait.

AGNES. Well, color me envious right about now.

KALIOPE. What troubles you, Agnes the Ass-hatted?

AGNES. I joined this adventure to get to know my sister, to help her, but I don't think she needs me at all.

KALIOPE. Well, I don't think she needs help from most people. She IS a 20th level Paladin after all.

If anything, we travel with her for we often require her help.

AGNES. Wow, Elf, you're really bad at giving advice.

KALIOPE. I apologize. Would you like to copulate with me now?

AGNES. What?

KALIOPE. Copulate, fornicate, consensual intimate stimulus. I think it would make you feel better. I hear you humans like to do such things.

AGNES. CHUCK! I'm not going to have sex with the Elf-girl!

CHUCK. What? I don't want to see you get sexy with the sexy Elf-girl. Why would I want to see that? Ew, gross, hot-girl on hot-girl action. Your sister must have wrote that out. I mean, that's so gay and I'm so…straight.

AGNES. Are you done?

> (**AGNES** *turns back to* **KALIOPE** *who leans in for a kiss.*)

Whoa, what are you doing?

KALIOPE & CHUCK. *(Whispers.)* Nothing!

AGNES. CHUCK!

CHUCK. Fine. Whatever.

You return back to your party who are all at the foot of the Mountain of Steepness. But before you can move forward, you spy something ahead of you. It's big, cube-shaped, and gelatinous!

> (*Lights come up on a gelatenous cube as the rest of* **AGNES**'s *part step up beside her.*)

AGNES. Ew, what is that?

KALIOPE. Oh that? That, my dear human friend, is Boss Number Two. Miles the Gelatinous Cube!

AGNES. What?

> (**ADVENTURER STEVE** *enters.*)

STEVE. It is I, the great Mage Steve and I've come to – oh neat, a jello mold!

> (**STEVE** *goes to touch The Gelatinous Cube, but it sucks him down whole…*)

Ahhhhh!

> (*…And spits out bones and his armor.*)

> (*The Cube burps.*)

AGNES. You made my boyfriend a jello-mold?

TILLY. What? No.

KALIOPE. You actually did.

LILITH. The Elf is correct, Love. You indeed made Agnes the Ass-Hatted's lover into a big cube of demonic gelatine.

ORCUS. So, hold up, that thing isn't edible?

KALIOPE. No.

ORCUS. Dammit, and I got the munchies!

AGNES. Why'd you make Miles a flesh-eating jello-mold?

TILLY. I don't know.

AGNES. Tilly!

TILLY. Maybe because he sucks.

AGNES. I thought you liked him.

TILLY. Yeah, I loved watching you two make-out everyday in our living room to that Cranberries CD.

AGNES. We weren't listening to the Cranberries. It was 10,000 Maniacs.

TILLY. Oh, I'm sorry, that's so much less lame.

AGNES. Whatever, he's my boyfriend!

TILLY. He's a fart-knocker.

AGNES. He liked you.

TILLY. He touched me.

(Shocked silence.)

AGNES. What?

(Still shocked. Still silent.)

TILLY. Okay, no, he didn't. But he mighta.

AGNES. That's not funny!

TILLY. "That's not funny."

AGNES. Seriously, that's not something to joke about.

TILLY. "Seriously, that's not something to joke about."

AGNES. Real mature.

TILLY. "Real mature."

AGNES. Stop that!

TILLY. "Stop that!"

> *(**LILITH** steps in between the two squabbling sisters.)*

LILITH. Though I find you mocking your sister incredibly sexy, shouldn't we, you know, kill this thing before it kills us.

TILLY. You're right. Okay, team, let's kill Miles!

AGNES. Wait. No.

TILLY. See, and once again, you're choosing your boyfriend over me.

KALIOPE. Your boyfriend is a gelatinous cube? Gross.

ORCUS. Ya know what? I'd do it.

What? It might feel good. It's slick.

AGNES. This isn't fair, Tilly, and you know it.

TILLY. I thought you were here to save my soul. I guess you didn't mean it. Quest is over, guys! We lost. The last adventure I will ever take ended in a forfeit!

AGNES. Stop.

TILLY. Why? So I can watch you run off and move in with Slimy McSlimerface over there and forget all about me?

AGNES. I would never forget about you.

TILLY. You did when I was alive.

*(This comeback cuts **AGNES** deep.)*

ORCUS. Oh snap, she went there!

TILLY. So are we giving up or what?

*(**AGNES** regains her composure.)*

AGNES. Fine. Whatever. It's clearly not my boyfriend, right? You just named him that. Miles isn't actually green, slimy, and cube-shaped.

LILITH. So are we going to kill it or not?

AGNES. Fine. Let's fight it.

TILLY. Really?

AGNES. Really.

TILLY. Alright! You hear that, Miles! We're gonna kill the crap out of you and your dumb face!

AGNES. Can we not call it Miles?

TILLY. Sure. I don't have to call it Miles.

(Suddenly the Gelatinous Cube magically transforms into the actual human **MILES**. *Except this* **MILES** *dressed like Conan the Barbarian and armed with a large broadsword.)*

AGNES. What the hell?

TILLY. Oh, I don't think Boss number two was actually a gelatinous cube.

LILITH. It's a shape-shifter.

KALIOPE. A doppelganger to be exact.

TILLY. So go kill it, sis. Yay!

*(***TILLY*** *pushes* **AGNES** *forward.)*

CHUCK. BOSS FIGHT NUMBER TWO: AGNES VERSUS MILES THE DOPPELGANGER!!!

AGNES. You're not actually him – you're not actually him.

MILES. Hey, baby, how ya doing? Have you finished packing the apartment just yet?

AGNES. Uh, not yet.

*(***MILES*** *takes a swing at her. She dodges.)*

MILES. Well, get to it!

AGNES. This is not fair, Tilly!

TILLY. It's a boss, it's not supposed to be fair.

AGNES. You're not actually Miles.

MILES. Don't tell me who I am!

*(***MILES*** *takes another large swing at her.* **AGNES** *dodges it last minute, but falls to the ground. She's now on her bum.)*

AGNES. Seriously, are you guys not going to help?

LILITH, KALIOPE, ORCUS, TILLY. *(Ad-libbing.)* No, not really. You look like you got it handled. I don't want to step in between a lovers' fight. It's really none of my business.

AGNES. You guys suck.

MILES. Hey, baby, since you're down there, why don't you say hi to my little friend.

(He gives her a smirk.)

(He then suddenly takes a final swing at her, this time she blocks his blade with her own.)

AGNES. Actually, asshole, I don't care who you look like, nobody disrespects me!

*(Back on her feet, **AGNES** attacks **MILES**. Their blades clash back and forth in an impressive array of swordplay. With her smaller weapon, **AGNES** is able to attack quickly, putting **MILES** in a defensive posture.)*

*(However when he gets a swing in, his heavier sword knocks **AGNES** blade clear out of her hands.)*

(He takes a few swipes at her while she's defenseless, she luckily avoids most of them, except for one that slashes her in the arm.)

Ahh!

*(He tries to stab her through, but overcommits his attack. **AGNES**'s disarms him.)*

*(**AGNES** now rears back a punch to hit him.)*

MILES. You can't hurt me. I'm wearing armor.

AGNES. Good point.

*(**AGNES** kicks **MILES** in the junk.)*

(He keels over. She breaks his neck.)

(He dies.)

TILLY. Wow. And I was just starting to like that guy. Too bad. Let's go.

Scene Thirteen

(EVIL **TINA** *and* **EVIL GABBI** *enter. Except they aren't evil this time; they're just students. No wings or horns or bloody mouths, just regular cheerleaders. And they're super chipper and nice.)*

EVIL TINA. Hello, Miss Evans!

EVIL GABBI. Do you have a moment?

AGNES. Uh. Sure.

EVIL TINA. We're selling ads for this year's yearbook and we wondering if you'd be interested in buying an ad?

AGNES. Why would I want to do that? I'm not selling anything.

EVIL GABBI. It doesn't have to be a literal ad.

EVIL TINA. It could just be a "Congratulations to the Class of '95!"

EVIL GABBI. Or an encouraging message to your graduating students.

EVIL TINA. Or a dedication to a loved one who *would* be graduating this year...

EVIL GABBI. *(Whispers.)* TINA!

EVIL TINA. *(To* **GABBI**.*)* Shhh.

    (To **AGNES**.*)*

So what do you think?

AGNES. You were in the same class as my sister, right?

EVIL TINA. Yes.

EVIL GABBI. Me and Tina loved her.

EVIL TINA. She was...such a good spirit. Wouldn't you agree, Gabbi?

EVIL GABBI. Totally. She always knew how to make someone smile.

EVIL TINA. We were both just devastated when it happened. I mean we didn't hang out after school a lot, but –

EVIL GABBI. We'd both consider her a very close friend.

AGNES. Is that right?

EVIL TINA. Not to be too bold, but I think buying a full page ad for Tilly would be…just amazing.

EVIL GABBI. We could even help you with it?

AGNES. Oh yeah?

EVIL TINA. I write poetry.

EVIL GABBI. And I draw.

EVIL TINA. We could put something nice in there for her.

EVIL GABBI. What do you think?

AGNES. Can I see your yearbook there?

EVIL TINA. Of course.

> (**AGNES** *violently throws it against the walls. The pages fly everywhere.*)

AGNES. GET THE HELL OUT OF MY CLASSROOM!!!

EVIL TINA. Yes, ma'am.

EVIL GABBI. Sorry to bother you!

> (*The two girls run out.*)

> (**TILLY** *enters.*)

TILLY. That seemed really effective.

AGNES. What am I supposed to do, Tilly? I can't beat up students.

TILLY. I woulda.

AGNES. …

TILLY. Agnes…

AGNES. …

TILLY. Agnes…

AGNES. …

TILLY. Are you still mad at me for making you kill your boyfriend?

AGNES. That trick was really uncool.

TILLY. Miles is really uncool.

AGNES. I love him.

TILLY. Then how come you're not married to him?

AGNES. I'm twenty-four, I don't need to be married.

TILLY. Yeah, but twenty-four in Ohio-time is like geriatric, it's like super old, it's like thirty. Shouldn't you already have a kid? Or two?

AGNES. Well, it doesn't matter, 'cause neither one of us is ready.

TILLY. Whatever you say...

> (**AGNES** *stares at the ghost of her sister standing there.*)

AGNES. Am I going crazy?

TILLY. Hey, it's better than being dead.

Scene Fourteen

AGNES. So where were we?

CHUCK. Let me see…

You and your party are climbing the Mountain of Steepness when suddenly you run back into…

(MILES enters.)

MILES. Hey.

CHUCK. Your boyfriend? No, that's not right.

AGNES. Hey.

MILES. Am I interrupting anything?

CHUCK. Well, sorta.

MILES. Were you guys playing… Dungeons and Dragons?

AGNES. Yeah.

MILES. Cool.

AGNES. We weren't having kinky Dungeon sex if that's what you were wondering.

CHUCK. What? That was an option?

AGNES. No.

MILES. Vera told you, huh?

AGNES. Yep.

MILES. I misinterpreted.

AGNES. With a high schooler?

MILES. Well, he is really big for his age.

CHUCK. I'm not big. Maybe you're just small. In the pants.

MILES. What?

CHUCK. Nothing!

MILES. Are you mad at me?

AGNES. I'm not happy.

MILES. Okay, that's fair, but you're not mad.

AGNES. Well, keep asking that question and we'll see.

MILES. Well, I came by because I thought, maybe, we could go back to OUR new place and start unpacking some boxes.

AGNES. I'm still not finished packing Tilly's room.

MILES. No, what I'm saying is maybe we can go back…to OUR new place and, you know, do some unpacking. I have something special planned that you might like.

AGNES. Like what?

MILES. Like…special.

CHUCK. I think he's implying sex.

AGNES. Thank you, Chuck.

CHUCK. But the unpacking analogy is really confusing.

AGNES. I'm busy, Miles.

MILES. You're just playing a game.

AGNES. It's more than that.

MILES. Can it not wait for just one night?

AGNES. No.

MILES. Well, okay, how about Friday? Can we hang out on Friday?

AGNES. I don't know…

MILES. I thought you said you weren't mad.

AGNES. I'm not mad. I'm just focused on this right now.

MILES. Baby, come on.

AGNES. I'm not in the mood for –

CHUCK. Hey, do you want to play?

MILES. What?

AGNES. Huh?

CHUCK. Yeah, you should play. I mean if you want to hang out, let's hang. I mean you can't do any worse than Agnes here, right? She sucks.

AGNES. He doesn't want to play.

(**MILES** *looks at* **CHUCK,** *the game, and* **AGNES.**)

MILES. Actually, I would. I would like to play, Chuck.

AGNES. What are you doing?

MILES. This is important to you and I want to be part of it.

AGNES. It's private though.

MILES. I know. But you never talk to me about Tilly or your parents or any of it. I just…if this could help me get to know you better, I wanna try. Please.

AGNES. You're for real?

MILES. I am.

> (**AGNES** *thinks it over…*)

AGNES. Fine. Roll him up a character sheet.

> (**CHUCK** *rolls dices as* **TILLY, KALIOPE, LILITH,** *and* **ORCUS** *enter.*)

LILITH. Agnes, look out!

KALIOPE. Boss Number Two!

AGNES. It's okay!

ORCUS. Dude, if that thing is that hard to kill, I give up now.

AGNES. NO! This is not Boss Number Two. This is Miles, the real Miles, my boyfriend.

TILLY. What's he doing here?

AGNES. He wanted to come.

TILLY. We already have five people in our party.

AGNES. He wants to get to know you – us – better.

TILLY. It's not really the same thing, now is it?

ORCUS. 'Bout time we got some more testosterone into this estrogen party. What's up? I'm Orcus, resident "horny dude."

MILES. So this is Dungeons and Dragons, huh? Neat.

TILLY. You're not serious.

AGNES. Look, you may not like him, but at least I know he has my back.

TILLY. We have your back.

AGNES. Right, just like last time when you made me KILL MY BOYFRIEND?

MILES. You killed me?

AGNES. No, I just killed a big fat blob that looked like you.

MILES. I look like a big fat blob?

TILLY. If you got in trouble, we would have stepped in.

KALIOPE. Assuredly.

LILITH. I wouldn't have.

ORCUS. No way.

TILLY. Guys, you're not helping.

AGNES. So what's the next thing we have to fight?

KALIOPE. The next boss is a Beholder.

AGNES. Aw, that sounds cute. Like "Beauty is in the eye of…"

> (*TILLY, KALIOPE, ORCUS, and LILITH look at each other.*)

TILLY, KALIOPE, ORCUS, LILITH. (*Ad-libbing.*) No. Nope. Not the same thing at all. That thing is ugly. Like just one big scary eyeball with teeth ugly.

MILES. Trust me, babe. Whatever it is, we're going to be fine. I'm here now.

> (*Explosion!!!*)

> (*The SUCCUBI are back.*)

> (*TILLY, KALIOPE, ORCUS, LILITH, and AGNES all fall into defensive stances as MILES just stands there.*)

EVIL GABBI. Oh my God, Evil Tina, look! An impenetrable wall of gay.

EVIL TINA. How will we ever get passed them?

AGNES. Miles, get back!

MILES. Why?

TILLY. Get back behind us, dummy!

MILES. Guys, they're just two cute little girls. What are they going to do?

> (*EVIL TINA and EVIL GABBI let out a little cute schoolgirl laugh…*)

EVIL TINA & EVIL GABBI. Heeheehee!

> (*…And then rips out his heart.*)

> (*MILES falls to the ground dead.*)

EVIL TINA. Yummy, I was looking for a snack.

TILLY. Well, he didn't last long.

(AGNES grabs TILLY by the arm.)

AGNES. Tilly, shoot them with a magic missile.

TILLY. I can't.

AGNES. What do you mean you can't?

TILLY. I forgot the spell.

AGNES. What do you mean you forgot the spell?

TILLY. It's a thing. A D&D thing. It's not going to help us.

(The SUCCUBUS twins begin circling their prey.)

EVIL GABBI. How hungry are you, Evil Tina?

EVIL TINA. Starving.

EVIL GABBI. What would you like first? Light or dark meant?

EVIL TINA. I'm in the mood for…geek.

(They both start towards TILLY.)

LILITH. I suggest we stop these succubi the old fashion way.

AGNES. And that would be?

LILITH. With violence, love. Lots and lots of violence.

(They all raise their weapons.)

EVIL ANGEL. Oh no, what will we fight them with?

EVIL TINA. We're so unarmed.

*(Suddenly, **ADVENTURER STEVE** arrives on the scene with two long blades in each hand.)*

STEVE. It is I, the great Mage Steve, returned to do battle with…oh, hello ladies.

(The SUCCUBI rip off STEVE's arms and take his weapons. He obviously dies. Again.)

EVIL TINA. I guess that answers that.

(TILLY's party attacks. A huge fight ensues.)

(The evil SUCCUBI eventually corner TILLY.)

Awww, look at the little nerd girl.

EVIL GABBI. Are you going to pee your pants, nerd girl?

EVIL TINA. Don't worry, dyke, your pain is about to end!

> *(**EVIL TINA** rears back her sword to strike down* **TILLY.***)*

> *(Seeing her love in trouble,* **LILITH** *rushes over to protect her!)*

LILITH. No!

> *(However as she rushes them, the* **SUCCUBI** *easily avoid her desperate attack and stab her through.)*

> *(Looking at the open wound on her torso,* **LILITH** *falls to the ground motionless.)*

TILLY. LILITH!!!

EVIL TINA. Awww, did your girlfriend just die?

EVIL GABBI. Aw, that's so sad. Aren't they just so sad?

> *(They both laugh mockingly at* **TILLY** *and the dead* **LILITH.***)*

> *(**AGNES, KALIOPE,** and **ORCUS** get back on their feet.)*

ORCUS. I don't see what's so funny.

AGNES. You'll just be joining her in two seconds.

KALIOPE. Prepare to be ushered to your deaths.

EVIL TINA. You can't hope to beat us.

EVIL GABBI. We're way too powerful for you.

> *(**AGNES** steps forward.)*

AGNES. Who said we were going to do it with our fists?

> *(The smirks on the* **SUCCUBI***'s faces suddenly disappear.)*

EVIL TINA. What do you mean?

> *(**AGNES** tosses away her sword and shield.)*

AGNES. Enough with all this dorky swordfighting stuff –

> *(She begins applying on some lipstick.)*

You really think you're badasses? Then let's finish this...

(She sticks out her hands as **KALIOPE** *and* **ORCUS** *puts pom-poms into them.)*

Cheerleader style.

We challenge you...to a dance battle.

(Lightning and thunder!!!!)

CHUCK. BONUS ROUND: AGNES, THE ELF, AND ORCUS VERSUS THE EVIL **SUCCUBI** CHEERLEADERS!!!

(Music like C&C Music Factory's "Gonna Make You Sweat"* fills the house as the two crews go at it in a full-on cheerleader'esque dance battle.)

*(***AGNES***'s crew starts it out. They look good... comedic and funny, but still good.)*

(The two **SUCCUBI**, *unimpressed, step up and start doing an elaborate cheerleading/hip-hop fusion routine that completely kills it. It's truly truly truly outrageous.)*

(Thinking they've won, the **SUCCUBI** *raise their arms in victory. When they do,* **AGNES** *and company pick up their weapons and drive it through their unsuspecting enemies.)*

EVIL TINA. No fair!

EVIL GABBI. You cheated.

*(***AGNES** *smiles coyly.)*

AGNES. What? You really thought we were gonna dance battle you to death. Wow, I guess my sister's right. Cheerleaders *are* dumb.

*(***AGNES** *kills them both.)*

---

*A license to produce *She Kills Monsters* does not include a performance license for "Gonna Make You Sweat." The publisher and author suggest that the licensee contact ASCAP or BMI to ascertain the rights holder to acquire permission for performance of this song. If permission is unattainable, the licensee should create an original composition in a similar style. For further information, please see music use note on page 3

(AGNES turns back to TILLY and the fallen LILITH.)

(Seeing TILLY cry over LILITH is too much for her.)

AGNES. Can we resurrect her?

KALIOPE. No. Tillius used that spell to save you.

AGNES. But you're magical, do something.

KALIOPE. I don't have that kind of magic.

AGNES. Orcus?

ORCUS. I only keep souls. I don't put them back.

AGNES. CHUCK!

(As if magically summoned, CHUCK and the gaming table suddenly appear.)

CHUCK. What?

AGNES. Bring her back.

CHUCK. I can't.

AGNES. You killed her girlfriend, now bring her back.

CHUCK. I didn't kill her. She jumped in the way. I rolled the dice, it says she died.

AGNES. Screw the dice, just bring her back!

CHUCK. I can't. Not for this adventure. There's rules.

AGNES. What rules?

You're the DM, you make the rules.

CHUCK. No, I don't. Gary Gygax makes the rules.

AGNES. Who the hell is Gary Gygax?

CHUCK. He's the ones who made the game.

AGNES. I don't care what you have to do, Chuck. Just bring her back. Now.

(The deceased MILES sits up from where he's been lying dead the whole time.)

MILES. Hey, babe. Um, maybe you should take a breather. I just died and I'm fine.

AGNES. No, I'm not going to let my sister just suffer like this.

MILES. It's not actually your sister.

AGNES. Screw you!

MILES. Babe.

AGNES. Are you going to bring her back?

CHUCK. I'm sorry.

AGNES. No! Wrong answer!

>   (**AGNES** *violently pushes all the D&D game pieces
>   off the table.*)

MILES. Agnes...

>   (**TILLY** *enters.*)

TILLY. Stop.

AGNES. Go away.

TILLY. They're right, you know.

AGNES. Shut up.

TILLY. It's just a game.

AGNES. I was getting to know you. I was just starting to get
to know you.

>   (**MILES,** *who can't hear* **TILLY***'s part of the
>   conversation, cautiously approaches.*)

MILES. Getting to know who, babe?

TILLY. My character's not dead.

AGNES. But you are.

TILLY & MILES. Agnes.

AGNES. This is a stupid game and you're not real and none
of this matters because you died.

TILLY & CHUCK. Agnes.

AGNES. Chuck, I'm done.

CHUCK. What?

AGNES. Thank you so much for indulging me.
Really.
It was...something.
I'll call you if I change my mind.
But I'm done talking to ghosts.
Good-bye.

Scene Fifteen

(VERA's office.)

(AGNES walks in.)

VERA. How's the packing coming along?

AGNES. It's alright, I guess.

VERA. Miles says you had a bit of a meltdown.

AGNES. When did you two become buddy-buddy?

VERA. He came by. Wanted my help on something.

Hey.

What's up?

AGNES. I'm just in a funk.

VERA. Agnes, it's me. I'm not your stupid man. Talk to me.

AGNES. It's dumb.

VERA. You're talking to the girl who has a Poison tattoo on her ass. I know stupid. I inked stupid on my butt. I'm sure whatever stupid you're doing ain't gonna cost you a thousand dollars in laser stupid removal.

AGNES. It was just that game was all I had of her.

Just a stupid character sheet and whatever she left scribbled out in that notebook.

VERA. That's not true – you have your memories –

AGNES. My memories? Right.

Do you want to know what my memories of Tilly are?

They're of this little nerdy girl who I never talked to, who I ignored, who I didn't understand because she didn't live in the same world as I did. Her world was filled with evil jello molds and lesbian demon queens and slacker Gods while mine...had George Michaels and leg-warmers.

I didn't get her. I assumed I would one day – that she'd grow out of all this – that I'd be able to sit around and ask her about normal things like clothes and TV shows and boys...and as it turns out, I didn't even know she didn't even like boys until my DM told me.

VERA. It's okay, Agnes.

AGNES. No, it's not.

> I didn't know her, Vera. I remember her as a baby, I remember her as this little toddler I loved picking up and holding, but I don't remember her as a teen at all. I'll never get the chance to know her as an adult.
>
> And now all I have left is this stupid piece of paper and this stupid made-up adventure about killing a stupid made-up dragon.

VERA. Agnes, baby…

> *(CHUCK appears at the door.)*

CHUCK. Agnes – I mean Miss Evans – um, do you have a moment?

AGNES. What are you doing here, Chuck?

CHUCK. I, um, wanted to return you this.

> *(CHUCK hands AGNES the module.)*

AGNES. Thank you.

CHUCK. I was also wondering if you were free this afternoon.

AGNES. Are you asking me out?

CHUCK. I can do that?

VERA. She was being sarcastic.

AGNES. What do you want, Chuck?

CHUCK. I just wanted to show you something. It's something of Tilly's.

AGNES. What?

> *(AGNES gets up and follows CHUCK.)*
>
> *(A door appears.)*
>
> *(CHUCK knocks on it.)*

> Where is this?

CHUCK. This is a friend's house.

AGNES. Who?

(The door opens, it's **ORCUS**...*just dressed as a normal High School kid though.)*

ORCUS. What's up, home-slice.

AGNES. Orcus?

CHUCK. Actually...this is Ronnie.

ORCUS. Hey, wow.

Older girl.

At my house.

Sweet.

CHUCK. I just wanted you to meet some of Tilly's friends. Ronnie, this is who I was telling you about.

ORCUS. Whoa, you're Tilly's sister?

CHUCK. Yeah.

ORCUS. You are a total Betty!

CHUCK. Dude.

ORCUS. What, dude?

CHUCK. Outside voice.

ORCUS. I'm saying stuff outloud I should just keep in my head again, right?

My bad.

Sorry.

CHUCK. So is your sister around?

ORCUS. Yeah. Lemme get her.

You guys can come in if you want, just don't touch the TV, I'm recording Power Rangers!

(They enter his house.)

AGNES. You really didn't do much to make him different. He's basically the same except not red...and straight.

*(***CHUCK*** takes a picture off a mantle and hands it to* **AGNES**.*)*

CHUCK. That's a picture of his sister.

*(***AGNES*** looks at it and realizes who it is...)*

AGNES. Kaliope.

CHUCK. Kelly, actually.

AGNES. Wow. Is she actually hotter in real life?

CHUCK. Yep.

AGNES. So what are you trying to show me here? That my sister was really good at drawing up her friends?

CHUCK. Not exactly.

> (RONNIE [ORCUS] returns with his sister. She walks in using fore-arm crutches to help stabilize her cerebral palsy.)

KALIOPE. What's up, Chuck?

CHUCK. Hey there, hot stuff!

KALIOPE. Who's this?

CHUCK. Tilly's sister.

KALIOPE. Oh, hi! Nice to meet you.

AGNES. Uh…hi.

> (Shocked, AGNES blatantly stares at KALIOPE's legs.)

KALIOPE. What? Do I have something on my shoes?

AGNES. (Suddenly embarrassed.) Oh God, I'm so sorry, I didn't mean to –

KALIOPE. It's okay. I'm used to it.

> (KALIOPE smiles at AGNES.)

> (AGNES returns it.)

AGNES. So you play D&D with these guys?

KALIOPE. Yeah, well. My brother's always been into it, but it was actually your kid sister that convinced me give it a shot. I know it's dorky, right?

AGNES. Yeah, I guess.

KALIOPE. Your sister was awesome, Miss Evans. We loved her. We really miss her.

AGNES. Me too.

> (TILLY enters.)

TILLY. What are you doing?

(AGNES turns to TILLY. As she does, the world behind her disappears.)

(The two girls are now in the middle of a dark void, only lit by two small pools of light.)

AGNES. I'm getting to know your friends.

TILLY. Are you judging them?

AGNES. No.

TILLY. I know they're geeky, I'm geeky, we're all geeks.

AGNES. Why do you think I care about that stuff?

TILLY. Everyone else does or did. I mean until I got hit by a car and then suddenly, wow, I'm the most popular girl in school.

AGNES. Is that why all you guys play this?

TILLY. No, we play it because it's awesome. It's about adventures and saving the world and having magic. And maybe – I guess – in some small teeny capacity, it might have a little to do with wish fulfillment. Kelly gets to walk without crutches, Ronnie gets to be super strong...

AGNES. What about you?

TILLY. Me?

I get the girl.

(Lights come up on the "real life" high schooler LILITH. AGNES approaches.)

AGNES. Hi.

LILITH. Hello, Miss Evans.

AGNES. Can we talk for a minute? I promise I'm not going to yell.

LILITH. Okay.

AGNES. Look, I'm sorry about that outburst in Miss Martin's office, but I was dealing with something.

LILITH. I get it.

AGNES. Look, I know you're not gay or was my sister's whatever, but she wanted you to have this. It's a letter she wrote to you.

LILITH. What does it say?

AGNES. It wasn't written to me. I don't know.

Do you want it?

LILITH. Yes.

> (**LILITH** *immediately opens it and reads it to herself.*)
>
> (*When she's done, she looks up to* **AGNES.** *Her eyes are now full of tears.*)

Thank you, Miss Evans.

AGNES. Have a good day.

LILITH. Wait.

AGNES. Yeah?

LILITH. I, uh… I did know Tilly.

AGNES. I know. You were at her funeral.

LILITH. No, I mean…we were close.

I mean, she wasn't my girlfriend or anything, but I always knew she was, you know, interested.

And, well, maybe I could have been too, it's just I didn't know…well, I don't know.

Anyways, you're not crazy. Tilly was my first kiss. I'm pretty sure I was hers too. I thought you'd might want to know that about your sister.

AGNES. Thank you for telling me.

LILITH. And Miss Evans –

I did love her.

I just wish I could have told her that.

AGNES. Yeah, I know what you mean.

> (**LILITH** *smiles, gets up, and walks away with tears now freely falling down her face.*)
>
> (*To herself.*)

Okay, Chuck, I get it.

Let's do this.

Scene Sixteen

(ORCUS, KALIOPE, *and* TILLY *suddenly are all standing beside* AGNES.)

(CHUCK *is back in his DM seat.*)

CHUCK. BOSS NUMBER THREE!!!!

(*All the fighters draw their weapons.*)

VERA THE BEHOLDER!!!

(VERA *the beholder, a ferocious single eye-balled monster with sharp sharklike teeth, floats into the space.*)

VERA. PUNY ADVENTURERS! YOU HAVE NO HOPE TO DEFEAT ME! I AM A BEHOLDER!!! AND I WILL –

(AGNES *walks up and simply stabs it in the eye.*)

(*It dies.*)

AGNES. Well, that was super easy.

(AGNES *turns back to her team.*)

So where's this dragon Tiamat?

This is the right Castle of Evil, right?

TILLY. It's the right castle.

AGNES. So where is it?

TILLY. Well, Agnes, there's something you should know about Tiamat.

AGNES. What?

TILLY. It's a shapeshifter.

ORCUS. Like Miles the Gelatinous Cube.

AGNES. Okay?

KALIOPE. So it can take any form.

TILLY. A friend.

ORCUS. A lover.

KALIOPE. Anybody.

(STEVE *enters.*)

STEVE. It is I, the great mage Steve!

> (*AGNES pulls out a knife and throws it at* **STEVE**. *It slams into his head and kills him instantly.*)

AGNES. Take that, you…dragon?

> (**STEVE** *does not move.*)

He's, um, not getting back up.

KALIOPE. He's not Tiamat.

AGNES. If he's not then who is?

> (*From a long staircase, the shadow of a dark warrior slowly enters the room.*)

> (*It's their supposed dead-friend* **LILITH**.)

LILITH. I don't know, love. Where could you possibly find a monster in this game?

AGNES. Lilith?

LILITH. I mean, look around, where oh where can all the monsters be?

> (*Looking around,* **AGNES** *starts to realize that all the "heroes" she's been with have been traditional D&D monsters all along.*)

> (**TILLY** *pulls* **AGNES** *back and points at* **ORCUS***!*)

TILLY. Watch out, Agnes! Demon!

> (**ORCUS** *however accusingly points at* **KALIOPE***!*)

ORCUS. Oh no, a dark elf!

> (*In kind,* **KALIOPE** *points at* **LILITH**.)

KALIOPE. A Demon Queen!

> (**AGNES** *raises up her sword between herself and her former companions. However they all turn to* **AGNES** *and* **TILLY** *and slowly raise their fingers at* **AGNES***'s little sister.*)

LILITH, ORCUS, KALIOPE. Tiamat.

> (*Hearing this,* **AGNES** *turns to catch eyes with* **TILLY**.)

(TILLY is giving her a devilish grin.)

TILLY. What? You didn't actually think I was a paladin, did you? Everyone knows paladins can't shoot magic missiles.

(Clearly, AGNES did not know this...)

AGNES. Sure. Yeah. Everybody knows... WHAT?

(TILLY lets out a laugh. However it's deep and demonic. This scares AGNES.)

Um, Tilly, what's happening?

TILLY. What do you think is happening, "Big Sis"? This is a D&D adventure. And what would a D&D adventure be if you didn't get to fight a dragon?

(TILLY hands AGNES her sword.)

AGNES. Um... Chuck?

CHUCK. FINAL FIGHT! AGNES VERSUS TIAMAT!!!

(STEVE now rises to feet and joins the other four evil adventurers.)

(They all give evil grins as they walk backwards into the shadows.)

(AGNES is alone.)

(Suddenly, the world goes black.)

(Then there's footsteps. Large, heavy footsteps.)

(In the darkness, the screech of something large and reptilian screams out.)

(And then there's eyes. Giant bright red glowing eyes. Five sets of them.)

(From the dark fog and haze, Tiamat emerges from the shadows. The stage is filled with smoke.)

AGNES. Oh God.

(Suddenly Tiamat attacks! AGNES leaps out of the way and strikes out at the giant beast.)

(She slashes it in the neck, face, and body, which only sends sparks flying. Her strikes do nothing against it.)

(Tiamat flails its wings at her. One of them strikes her, sending **AGNES** *flying across the room like a rag-doll. She slams into a wall and then onto the ground. She's clearly out of her league.)*

(Tiamat snaps at her. She uses her shield from being bitten, but as she gets occupied fighting one head, another slings in and strikes her in the ribs.)

(They bite at her, grabbing onto her limbs. They breath fire [or compressed air] at her.)

(She shields herself for the fire and kicks away at the snapping heads.)

(The large beast and **AGNES** *wage an all out war against one another. It's an impressive and spectacular fight.)*

(And in the greatest fight ever to be seen on a theatrical stage, **AGNES** *summons the strength to survive. She plunges her sword deep into the heart of the beast.)*

(It rears back all of its heads into the air in anguish as it thrashes around in a loud, and explosive death.)

(The dragon finally collapses onto the stage dead.)

(However...it's not over.)

(From the smoke and shadows, a new figure slowly emerges.)

(Seeing it, **AGNES** *picks up her blade to defend herself until she sees who it is.)*

(It's **TILLY**. *The real* **TILLY**. *Now dressed like her little sister instead of the warrior princess.)*

(Seeing this, AGNES's eyes begin to fill with tears as her little sister approaches.)

TILLY. Good job.

AGNES. Tilly?

TILLY. So did you have fun?

AGNES. What?

TILLY. Did you have fun? That's the point in all this. Did you have fun?

(AGNES, not knowing how to respond, simply nods her head.)

Good.

(TILLY begins to exits.)

AGNES. Wait.

You're not real. You're gone.

TILLY. But this story remains. And isn't that essentially all that life is – a collection of stories? This is one of mine…

KALIOPE. …and not just some story that I experienced like a party or a dance or an event, but something I dreamt –

LILITH. Something far more personal and important than happenstance. This story came from my soul and by breathing life into it, who knows?

ORCUS. Maybe a bit of my soul gets the chance to breathe for a moment once again.

CHUCK. *(Reading from the module.)* I love you, my sister.

TILLY. I'm sorry I can't be there.

CHUCK. *(Reading from the module.)* I have no idea why you had to experience this adventure alone without me. But I hope it gave you a glimpse into me the way I wanted you to see me –

ORCUS. Strong…

LILITH. Powerful…

KALIOPE. And magical.

CHUCK. *(Closing the module.)* Congratulations, you have finished the Quest for the Lost Soul of Athens.

  (**TILLY** *and* **AGNES** *finally hug.*)

NARRATOR. And so… Agnes the Ass-hatted accomplished her very first quest. Soon she would embark on another and then another and so forth and so on for the rest of her life. Miles the boyfriend who would soon become Miles the fiancé and finally Miles the husband and father would join her on her many quests alongside Chuck the Big Brain'd and Tilly's old group of friends, Ronnie the Slacker, Kelly the not-so-good-legged, and Lilly the Closeted. Tilly was never forgotten, Agnes got married, and eventually the world finally embraced geeks not as outsiders, but as awesome. Agnes moved out of that old house and brought the many memories of an average life with her. And this made her happy.

  (*Lights fade.*)

End of Play